DREAM BOY

DREAM BOY

BY:

SPENCER J. BUCHANAN

Charleston, SC
www.PalmettoPublishing.com

Dream Boy

First Edition

Paperback ISBN: 978-1-64990-230-6
eBook ISBN: 978-1-64990-740-0

Prologue

Winter Crow, his brother, and best friend ran as four knights on horseback angrily threw spears and shot arrows. They dodged and spun as weapons clattered to the ground around them. They finally lost them when they ran around a burning house and into a crack in a small mountain by their village.

Superlet was under attack. Three demons, Char, Back, and Loss, had appeared through orange portals with their armies and started slaughtering everything that moved. Winter Crow and his brother didn't even have time to prepare, only run. They had grabbed Winter Crow's friend and ran. The whole village was in danger and there was nothing holding back the monsters.

Char, Back, and Loss had always been mean and cruel. They had always wanted power and rule over everything and that is why they destroyed worlds when they started getting too powerful. Although Char, Back, and Loss were brothers, Char was purple, Back was blue, and Loss was red. Loss had always been the alpha of their small pack. Their parents were Alande and Freedin. Alande and Freedin were both well-known demons and Char, Back, and Loss wanted to be just like them.

Winter Crow's world was full of witches and wizards who performed magic and had powers. Their powers were hereditary, so everyone had some sort of power passed down from their parents. Winter Crow was a wizard and had grown up learning to use magic. He could basically do anything except bring people back to life. No one could do that. It was just something that even his village's combined powers weren't capable of.

Winter Crow's brother, Silver Ape, was two years younger than him. He was a wizard too, but he hadn't had as much practice as Winter Crow because their father had died just as Silver Ape was gaining full control of his powers. Silver Ape was given his name because he shined like silver and was big and muscly like an ape.

Winter Crow's best friend, Violet Moth, was a warlock. Warlocks are only slightly different than wizards. Warlocks could do a higher level of magic. Warlocks could summon upon spirits, tame monsters, and transform objects into entirely new objects. Wizards couldn't do any of that. He was named "Violet Moth" because his cloak was violet and he could fly in the air like a moth. They had been best friends ever since Winter Crow's dad had died. Violet Moth had comforted Winter Crow and kept him company. Winter Crow's mom had died in labor when giving birth to Silver Ape, so Silver Ape had never known his mom.

They lived on the planet "Superlet." Superlet was a planet 1 billion light years away from the solar system called, "The Milky Way." Superlet was filled with fruits, plants, and animals. The weather was always good here too.

This planet had about 100 villages full of magical creatures. There were villages specifically for witches or wizards, one was full of unicorns, two were tiny fairy towns, ten or fifteen were full of leprechauns and warlocks, one was for dragons, three were for phoenix and griffins, five or six for satyrs and fauns, some for nymphs and sprites, seven for centaurs, one for gnomes, but this one was the only one that contained a little bit of everyone.

Fifteen light years away was the planet "Zon." Zon was a planet of darkness and evil. Everyone on Superlet used to live there as slaves until there was a revolt lead by Winter Crow's great grandpa. It had been 103 years since they considered themselves free. Now, the three demon kings of Zon were here with plans to slaughter everyone. Winter Crow, Silver Ape, and Violet Moth crept out of their hiding place and into a clearing in-between two houses. They could see a witch attempting to fight off six hellhounds with her magic and a leprechaun running away with his pot of gold (leprechauns were so greedy).

They walked out a little farther only to trip over a body. It was a wizard. The wizard had a long gray beard and had two arrows sticking out of his back. Winter Crow didn't know him, but shed two tears. Winter Crow and his companions stepped out into the village square. It was chaos. Dragons blew fire at knights and gobbled up hellhounds. Unicorns were zapping knights with lightning bolts coming out of their horns and fairies were pummeling an ogre with rocks. Satyrs and fauns kicked and punched oni and ogres. Gnomes threw assorted items at goblins and zombies. The village people weren't winning though. Soldiers captured fairies and sprites in nets to be taken back to Zon and ogres were throwing boulders at wizards. Knights on horseback rode around the square whacking witches with their swords. Zombies and goblins surrounded dragons and took them to the ground. Oni and ogres threw clubs and spears at the griffins flying in the sky. Then Winter Crow saw the three demon kings across the battlefield, breathing fire at fairies and freezing little leprechauns.

Winter Crow surprised himself with what he did next. He yelled at the top of his lungs, "Leave the people alone!!" The three friends demonstrated a united front.

Every hellhound, knight, monster, ogre, oni, zombie, goblin, and demon on the battle field turned to look at their seemingly old and weak competition. "Get him!!" cried a knight and everyone charged after the wrinkled man and his friends. Winter Crow, his brother, and friend ran. Winter Crow tried to summon upon all his magic. Then, with a burst of strength, the wizard turned around and launched a giant fireball right at the front of the army. Twenty-six monsters were instantly turned to ashes. His brother and best friend stared at him. The army stopped and the three demons pushed forward through the crowd. They stared in awe at the wizard as Winter Crow conjured up a portal to a planet called, "Earth." Superlet wouldn't last, so the wizard, his brother, and friend needed a new world of magic. They needed a world that was already populated and had the potential to sustain their type of life.

"Don't let them escape!!" Loss commanded his army. The monsters threw their javelins and spears, but Winter Crow, Silver Ape, and Violet Moth had already disappeared into the portal to Earth.

Chapter 1

Jacob and Holly had just exited a baby store in the mall. They had searched everywhere for a crib and couldn't seem to find one. They were about to have a baby and had three months left until the baby was due. It was a boy and they were leaning towards the name Jameson because it had been Jacob's dad's name. Jacob looked at his wife with her brown hair blowing in a breeze. He believed she was beautiful, even when she was frustrated with their unsuccessful shopping.

The baby store they had just left had mostly sold bibs and feeding supplies. It had also sold a couple of different brands of diapers and a few baby toys. Holly had bought three bibs and some baby toys. The three bibs were all different colors. The first one was green and read, "Feed Me!" and the second was black with a dinosaur pictured on it and had, "Grandma's cute-a-saurus" written on it. The third bib was white with green spots on it. A yellow star was in the middle and around the star was cursive writing that said, "Mommy's Little Star!", though none of these items had been their goal.

They were just about to walk into another store when a strangely dressed man standing by the water fountains started waving at them to come over. Jacob whispered to Holly, "Just keep walking."

"Holly! Jacob! I need to talk to you!" the man yelled across the mall.

"How do you know our names? Who are you and what do you need?" Jacob questioned, starting to get defensive.

"There is no reason for fear. I have a message for you! I am Winter Crow! That is my name because I can see all, like a crow, and I am pure and clean, like winter snow freshly fallen on the ground." the man said as he walked over to the couple and stopped in front of them.

"Are you headed to a party?" Holly asked, "You're wearing a wizard's hat and a wizard's robe."

The man did, in fact, have a purple wizard's hat and cloak on. He was also wearing purple winkle pickers. "Actually, I am indeed a *real* wizard. This crib is for you." Winter Crow pointed over to a crib that Holly and Jacob hadn't noticed before.

"Ohhhhh. That explains the odd name." Holly realized aloud.

"Wizards and magic are real? You're really a wizard?" Jacob said disbelievingly.

"How did you know we needed a crib?" Holly asked.

"I didn't know for sure. I just found it in the middle of a store and decided to get it for you....... Of course, I got it for you. I know all!" the wizard joked.

"Well, then thank you for the crib!" Holly confirmed, thinking privately that there was no sense in being ungrateful. She remembered the old saying about not looking a gift horse in the mouth. Her own mom had taught her that.

"You are pregnant with a boy and you are going to name him Jameson. He will have powers. When he dreams, his dreams will come true. They will literally leap from his mind and into the real world, but he can learn to control them." the wizard said.

"How did you know we were going to name him Jameson?" Holly asked, still stuck on the initial revelation.

"Holly, I just answered that. I'm a wizard. I know and see all!" Winter Crow yelled.

"So, you're telling me that my boy will be a sort of super-hero?" Jacob asked disbelievingly.

"Basically, yes." the magical being assured them.

Jacob put his arm protectively around Holly as she began to look woozy.

"Okay. Why are you telling us this?" Holly whispered.

"I'm telling you this because bad men will come after Jameson and it will put you all three in danger. They will want to use him to gain money and riches. He can dream once and they will receive everything they want. After they are done with him, they could kill him." the wizard said.

"Okay… But Jameson can protect us because he can control his dreams, right?" Holly asked.

"Yes, but just in case, as he learns, you may want to be pre-pared." the man said, and he handed Holly a dreamcatcher. The dreamcatcher was dark brown with white lace tied in it. It had brown and white feathers dangling at the bottom.

Holly asked, "Why do I need this? You know these don't really work. Dreamcatchers are simply decoration. They are rumored to catch bad dreams, but that's a bunch of bologna."

Winter Crow took out a hidden wand from his pocket and touched the dreamcatcher with it. "If you hang this in Jameson's bedroom, he will have only good dreams. It will help for a time until his 11th birthday. After that, he must learn to control his dreams." the wizard said.

Suddenly, the wizard disappeared with a flash of blue light. Holly and Jacob dazedly walked into the next baby store, wor-ried about their boy and his future. They believed the wizard and now they had to find a way to protect their son and their family.

Chapter 2

3 Months Later

"Drive!" yelled Holly, as she and Jacob raced to the hospital. "I'm going as fast as I can!" Jacob screamed at his panicked wife.

The hospital came into view and Jacob sped up. They reached the entrance to the building and rushed inside leaving their car right outside the door. The nurses immediately took Holly to a big room and then Jacob didn't see his wife again for about six hours.

....

Finally, after waiting so long that it hurt Jacob to think, two nurses walked over to his chair in the café. "Your wife has given birth to a baby boy. She is ready for you to come in if you would like." the first nurse said.

Jacob walked into his wife's room and sat down in a chair near the corner. A nurse stood by his wife taking notes and checking the monitors by the hospital bed. The nurse did her work diligently. The room smelled of roses. The rose smell was from the flowers on the table that Holly's parents had given her.

"Isn't he beautiful?" asked Holly as she rocked their baby in her arms and then carefully passed him to his father.

"He *is* beautiful." Jacob replied in a hushed tone, "Let's name him Jameson."

"That's what we planned, right?" Holly questioned.

"Yes. His name is Jameson." Jacob confirmed.

Jameson was one content baby. Jacob couldn't stop smiling down at his blue eyed and blonde-haired baby.

After a while, Jacob looked down at his watch, "It's 7pm. I need to go to Givensburg for an interview. I really need this new job. The working hours are better and I'll be home earlier each day with you and Jameson. I'm staying at the Sunny Side Hotel. I'll be back first thing tomorrow morning."

"That's fine. We will miss you, but we'll see you in the morning." Jacob's wife said.

"Do you have the dreamcatcher?" Jacob asked.

"No. I left it at home on accident in all the rush. I'm sure Jameson will be fine this first night." Holly said as she closed her eyes.

"I love you. Bye." Jacob said as he kissed his wife and walked out the door after tucking Jameson safely into his wife's arms and side.

"I love you too. Bye." Holly whispered as she and her baby drifted to sleep.

Unfortunately, sleeping meant dreaming and that night Jameson dreamt of a monster, a one-eyed monster.

Chapter 3

The next morning, Holly woke up to the sound of screaming in her hospital hallway.

She climbed out of her bed and laid her sleeping baby firmly between two pillows. She peeked out her door window only to see a doctor being thrown down the hallway by an enormously tall creature.

The beast had short black hair and very hairy legs and arms. It was wearing gray ripped shorts and a very muddy green shirt. The scariest thing about it was the one, very large, brown eye, perfectly centered in the middle of his head. It also had a giant axe in its hand.

She watched doctors and nurses calling police from their rooms or trying to attack the monster with assorted items only to be smashed or eaten by the humongous beast. There was a huge fire in the waiting room and a smaller one in the room across from Holly.

Holly rushed from her door to the window opposite on the wall looking outside. Then she saw a familiar car pull into the parking lot and her husband, Jacob, hopped out of it. Jacob walked inside and beheld a gruesome sight. Jacob ran to his wife's room and locked their door behind himself.

"What's going on?" Jacob yelled in a worried tone, "Is that a cyclops I saw?"

"Yes!! I think it's one of Jameson's dreams!" Holly screamed. She didn't know why she believed this was the case, but she just felt in her bones that it was true.

"None of those people can take the cyclops down. I'll have to help them!" Jacob shouted as he ran out the door.

"Jacob, no!" Holly yelled desperately.

"Hey, Mr. Ugly! Over here!" Jacob shouted as he swung a metal pipe he had picked up off the ground.

"Huh? Yay!! Another yummy creature!" The cyclops yelled.

"Jacob, run!" Holly screamed from the cracked doorway as she saw the cyclops lift his weapon.

Jacob heard Holly's cry and rolled sideways, just dodging the giant's axe.

Jacob leaped onto the monster and whacked the cyclops on the head with the pipe. The beast roared with pain and threw Jacob against the wall. Jacob laid on the floor, breathing heavily and holding his arm. Holly realized that Jacob's arm was broken.

The giant's head was bleeding and had a big gash on it. The cyclops roared and pounded the ground with his axe, creating cracks in the white tile.

"Jacob, get up!" Holly screamed when she saw the cyclops raise his axe once more, but it was too late.

The back of the cyclops's axe came right down on Jacob just as he stood back up and he plopped down, not moving, on the floor. The smoke from the fires finally reached the sprinklers and water started squirting everywhere. Just as the water hit the cyclops, he turned to golden dust.

Right at that very moment, Jameson woke up and started crying.

Holly ran over and cradled her baby in her arms. When she walked back over to the door, the police and fire department arrived and started bringing injured people to vacant rooms.

Holly opened her room door and ran over to her lifeless husband and wept. She was released from the hospital later the next day and went home with her baby to prepare a funeral and to mourn.

The only thing she wondered about was what would happen to her child and how she was going to be able to train him and help him alone.

Chapter 4

11 Years Later

Jameson was crawling out of bed when he heard the oven timer go off. He dressed quickly and walked into his kitchen. It smelled of freshly baked pancakes and bacon cooked by his mother.

Holly and Jameson lived in the town of Weston, Pennsylvania. It was a small town where everyone knew each other. If you went to the grocery store, you would know at least half of the people in the store. Jameson had blonde hair and blue eyes, which he had kept since his birth. He had freckles on his face running from the top of his cheeks to the top of his nose. Today, he was wearing a blue t-shirt and blue jeans. He was also wearing a blue and yellow Weston Wildcats baseball cap. Jameson played little league baseball and was pretty good at it.

Jameson had just celebrated his birthday two days ago with a giant pool party. He had invited all of his friends and family. He received everything he had asked for except for a dog. Jameson had always wanted a dog, but Jameson's mom didn't want to have to pay for food and water. Another reason she didn't want a dog was because Jameson and Holly were always gone during the day and no one would be at home to play with the animal.

Jameson's uncle had helped he and his mom get back on their feet after Jameson's dad died. His uncle had given them money and a roof over their heads until they found a home. Jameson didn't see his uncle very often, but he always loved when he did come to visit. Jameson was pretty close to his uncle. They liked the same things, played the same games, and engaged the same hobbies. Jameson's uncle also told Jameson stories about his dad. Uncle Andrew said that Jacob had been a very brave, strong, funny, hard-working man. He had also said that Jacob had been really fun to be around because he would tell jokes and make you smile every time. Uncle Andrew was Holly's brother and the siblings had always been really close.

The house they were living in was two stories, but included an attic and basement. Jameson's bedroom and his bathroom along with an extra guest bedroom were on the 2nd floor. Jameson's room was big! He had a loft bed with a desk, TV, bookshelf, and couch under it. He had a large toybox in the corner with all his action figures and bouncy balls. Jameson's bed had blue and gray sheets on it and his stuffed animals were neatly lined on his pillows. Jameson's dreamcatcher from his mom was hung from his nightlight at the end of his bed. Jameson loved his dreamcatcher because he believed it actually helped him only have good dreams. The ground level story had his mom's master bedroom, a large kitchen, the dining room, the living room, the laundry room, and the small bathroom by the kitchen. His favorite part of their house was the giant painting in the living room that had a bright orange sunset behind he and his mom. An artist had painted it for them when they had gone to the Grand Teton National Park in Wyoming. They had gone to the local elk refuge and asked for a painting of themselves and the sunset. The painting had a gold frame and was hung right above the big brown couch. When Jameson had watched a scary movie or his mind was unsettled, this picture was what he thought of when he fell asleep.

They had a large yard with a pool and outdoor kitchen that they used when they had a lot of guests over (which had been very often lately since it was near Christmas). Jameson loved swimming and swam every day in the pool, no matter the weather.

Right now, his living room had a large decorated tree in the corner with lots of ornaments and garland twinkling on it. Down their stairs, garland covered the rails. They had one happy snowman standing outside and snow piled all around their yard. Icicles lined the roof outside the house and all the trees were bare.

Jameson found himself a chair in the kitchen and started doing his math homework.

"Isn't that due today?" his mom asked as she passed him a stack of chocolate chip pancakes.

"Yes." Jameson replied, "But I didn't have time to do it yesterday because I had basketball practice."

"Ok. Eat up and get yourself to the road or you will miss the bus." Jameson's mom scolded.

Jameson thought his mom was awesome. She was organized and tidy. She was beautiful with long brown hair and shiny green eyes. She worked at the doctor's office down the road. She herself worked as a pediatrician and well-loved according to the good notes and reviews on the office's social media page. Every now and then she would find a fruit cake or pie from one of her patients laying on her desk.

Outside, the bus honked, and Jameson grabbed his backpack as he ran outside. He waved goodbye to his mom and stepped onto the bus headed to Weston Junior High.

Chapter 5

Second period was the worst. Jameson made a 68 on his fractions test and even tripped in front of the whole class when he was going to get his book that had fallen on the floor. Jameson was in 6th grade and was having a lot of trouble in his classes, especially math. Math made no sense!

The bell for his next class finally rang and Jameson bolted to his classroom. He loved his next class because it was his favorite subject, science, and because his science teacher Mrs. Jacky was super sweet and funny. Mrs. Jacky was his favorite because she gave everyone candy for their good grades. Sometimes it felt a little juvenile to work for candy, but Jameson liked it anyway.

Today was the science test that covered weathering, erosion, deposition and sedimentary rock. Jameson felt confident that he would make a 100 because he had studied all night previously with his mom.

After Mrs. Jacky passed out the tests, Jameson quickly answered the first 5 out of 20 questions of the test. Numbers 1-3 were about sedimentary rock and they just asked if it was made out of layers, where the rock was commonly found, and if it was made of sediments or big chunks of rock. Numbers 4-5 were about weathering and were also very easy. Jameson had trouble with numbers 10-17 because they asked about erosion which had been the most confusing thing for Jameson.

After the test was over, Mrs. Jacky called out the grades, "Jameson, 100!" That was the only grade Jameson needed to hear, but he was glad to hear Will's name called out with a 100, too.

Will was Jameson's best friend. They had been buddies since kindergarten. They had met on the monkey bars at the playground when Jameson fell off and hit the ground. Will jumped down to check on Jameson and they both ended up laughing until they couldn't breathe.

Carson, Brandon, and Jack were the meanest, rudest, cruelest kids in the 6th grade. They had kicked a dog on the side of the road near the grocery store on Saturday. Jameson knew because he had been shopping for milk at the time it happened. They shoved Will and Jameson's other friend, Rebekah, around like they were playing football. They had even put a tack in Mrs. Jacky's chair and had gotten away with it! Jameson had tried to stand up to them when they tripped Will at lunch on Friday, but they had shoved Jameson to the floor and sent him scrambling back to his table. They knew Jameson didn't like them and they had decided that they would make every one of Jameson's days terrible.

The bell for the end of the school day rang and everyone rushed to the buses and cars waiting in the parking lot.

Mrs. Jacky called Jameson to her desk just before he had gotten to the door, "Come here and let me give you your candy for that great 100 on your test! You and Will did fantastic!"

Mrs. Jacky reached into her black leather purse and gave Jameson a chocolate bar.

"Thank you!" Jameson yelled as he ran out the door and to the parking lot.

Jameson didn't know who was waiting for him until they had already pinned him down.

Chapter 6

Jameson walked outside to the buses and almost tripped when Brandon's foot popped out in front of him. Instead of tripping Jameson, Jameson accidentally tripped Brandon.

"You shouldn't have done that!" Brandon yelled as Carson and Jack closed in around Jameson from all sides.

Jameson knew he should scream for help, but he really wanted to punch Brandon right in the face. Instead, Jameson took off running towards the gym where Mr. Rogers, the gym teacher, would be working. Mr. Rogers would yell at them and send them to detention. The plan was perfect.

When Jameson ran, Brandon and his gang ran after Jameson as fast as they could. When Jameson got to the gym, Mr. Rogers was nowhere to be found. Jameson knew he was in trouble.

Jameson stopped on the concrete sidewalk in front of the gym door. He tried to open the door, but, of course, it was locked. He banged on the door, but he got no answer. Jameson heard running and laughing behind him and turned around to see Brandon, Carson, and Jack staring at him with murderous grins.

"Well, well, well, what do we have here? Did you really think you could get away from us? You're slower than my grandma! Hahaha!" Brandon said loudly as if trying to attract attention.

Jameson spotted a red and green poster on the outer wall of the gym. He knew that it had something to do with Christmas, but he didn't have time to look it over.

Jack and Carson started to close in on the right and Brandon on the left. Just as Brandon was about to throw a punch, the gym door swung open, knocking Jack and Carson onto the concrete.

Brandon stared in awe at Mr. Rogers standing in the doorway with a broom. "Great timing." Jameson thought to himself. Mr. Rogers had brown hair and wore black glasses. Today he was wearing an acorn brown suit and black tie. He looked good and smelled strongly of cologne. He was super nice and had a bright smile that always lit up the room.

Brandon didn't have time to run before Mr. Rogers smacked him with his broom, sending him toppling into Jack and Carson, who had just stood back up.

"We are so sorry, Mr. Rogers!" Brandon cried.

"We will never treat anyone like that again!" Carson yelled.

"Please, don't send us to detention!" Jack pleaded.

"Just because you said that, and that means you know you did wrong; I'm sending you to detention for three days!" Mr. Rogers said firmly.

"Nice going, wind bag!" Brandon yelled at Jack.

Brandon, Jack, and Carson ran like the wind to the car and bus lines before Mr. Rogers could give them another whack.

"Thanks, Mr. Rogers!" Jameson said as he hugged his P.E. teacher.

"Your welcome! I just can't understand why they bully you and your friends. They do it for no reason at all." Mr. Rogers said.

"You should have given them detention for three weeks." Jameson huffed.

"No. They have enough detention time. You should try to forgive them. I don't think they will bother you anymore." Mr. Rogers recommended.

"I'll try to talk to them next time I see them." Jameson said as he smiled.

"Good. Have you heard about the Jr. High Christmas Dance that's coming up?" Mr. Rogers asked.

"No. When is it?" Jameson replied.

"Just look at this poster." Mr. Rogers said as he pointed to the red and green poster Jameson had noticed earlier.

"The annual Christmas dance is at 5:00pm on Saturday. It will be in the junior high school gym and there will food, games, and music." Jameson read aloud.

"Yes. I hope to see you there. I will be chaperoning and working the concession stand. Now run along. You need to get home for dinner, and I need to sweep." Mr. Rogers stated as he waved Jameson along.

Chapter 7

Jameson waved goodbye to Mr. Rogers and ran to the car line. He hopped into the car, where his mom was waiting, and they drove home. Jameson wasn't hungry that night and decided to go to bed early at 6:00. His mom turned on a movie in her bedroom and also went to bed. She mentioned that she was tired too.

That night, Jameson's dream was terrible. He dreamt that he was at the upcoming dance with his friends Will, Rebekah, Meredith, and Cindy. They were whacking each other with glow sticks when one of the sticks broke and started sparking. Of course, Will grabbed it and threw it in the trash. Jameson told him not to because it would start a fire, but Will did it anyway.

Then Mr. Rogers called Jameson over to the concession stand and offered him a free coke because there were too many. Jameson ran back to his friends and they started dancing to the music. Soon, everybody joined in.

All was going great until the trash can Will had thrown the glow stick in, erupted in a column of flames.

Everyone gasped and screamed. The plastic trashcan melted and oozed onto some cardboard boxes by the snack stand. Immediately the boxes lit on fire, engulfing the concession stand and sending Mr. Rogers running outside screaming because he was on fire. The fire got so high that it lit the wooden ceiling on fire, sending timber and metal beams falling onto innocent kids.

Jameson and his friends screamed and ran as the fire continued to spread. They were almost to the door when a giant piece of wood fell, blocking the doorway. Everyone around Jameson screamed and panicked. They were all trapped, and they were all going to burn.

Suddenly, a screeching metal against metal sound went through the air. Jameson looked up just in time to see a beam falling from the ceiling straight at he and his friends. Jameson grabbed Meredith and Will and jumped forward. They crashed into two other kids, Becky and Carl. Jameson stood up and looked behind him at the beam laying on top of his friends, Rebekah and Cindy.

"No!" Meredith cried as she curled up in a ball on the floor.

"Why?!?" Will screamed, clearly shocked.

Jameson woke up crying. He wiped his tears away and looked at the clock. It read: 7:03 am. Jameson sat up and started to slide on his clothes for school. He brushed his teeth and grabbed a granola bar for a quick breakfast. He hummed on the ride to school, trying not to think about his horrible dream.

Chapter 8

School was great! Brandon, Carson, and Jack were in detention because they had chased Jameson around the school
the day before. Then in science the class earned free time as a
reward for all the good grades on the test. In math, Jameson
learned about decimals and really felt that the test over it would
be easy. Mr. Rogers was smiling and happy today in physical
education. He even let the students play dodgeball! All was
great, but Jameson couldn't stop thinking about his dream.

"Was it just a dream or was it really the future?" Jameson
wondered to himself.

Jameson pushed the thought aside and tried to focus on his
work. It was going to be a long day and he couldn't put all of
his attention on a stupid dream.

Jameson came home after school to see his mom in the
kitchen making his favorite meal, fried shrimp and french fries.
The shrimp were crusty and golden brown, and the french fries
were extra crunchy just like he preferred. He asked for some
ketchup for the fries and sat down to eat. After gobbling it up,
he asked for dessert. Dessert was dark chocolate chunk brownies and vanilla ice cream. The brownies and ice cream were
homemade and given to them by one of his mom's patients.

"You *have* to tell the lady who made these that they are
delicious." Jameson said with a mouthful of brownie.

"I promise I will the next time I see her." Holly said as she ate her last shrimp.

Jameson's mom stood up to get seconds. She grabbed some more shrimp and french fries and also poured herself some lemonade.

"So, Mom, I had a really weird dream last night..." Jameson said.

Jameson's mom dropped her plate and drink on the floor.

"Mom!!" Jameson yelled, "Are you okay?"

"Y-Yes. I'm fine." his mom replied, "W-What was your dream about?"

"Well, I was at the Christmas dance and the building caught on fire. A beam fell from the roof and killed Rebekah and Cindy." Jameson stated.

"Oh..." Jameson's mom looked scared.

"Mom?" Jameson said.

"W-What? Oh...I'm fine. Just tired. I'm headed to bed. Say your prayers and be sure to think of happier things before you get ready for bed." his mom warned.

Why was his mom acting so weird? Jameson didn't really care. He was tired too. Jameson brushed his teeth and fell quickly asleep.

Chapter 9

The following morning, Jameson woke up and got dressed immediately. Fortunately, he had no dreams that he could remember from last night. He made himself eggs and bacon for breakfast and turned on the television. His mom must have been sleeping in.

"Today is Saturday." Jameson said to himself.

"Today is Saturday!!" Jameson jumped up and gasped, "Today is the school dance. I hope my dream doesn't come true."

Jameson couldn't stop thinking about his dream now. What if it came true? What if his friends actually die and the gym really burns down?

Jameson spent his day watching TV, playing with his action figures, and relaxing in the hot tub. He was trying to keep himself busy, so he didn't think too much about the dream. Jameson got out of the pool, got dressed and brushed his teeth. He sat down on the couch and looked up at the clock. A wave of shock ran down his spine. It was 4:30pm and it was time to leave for the dance.

....

Jameson found his friends as soon as he stepped into the gym. They were over by the concession stand talking to Mr. Rogers.

Cindy wore a red dress and red shoes. Cindy also had red lip-stick on her lips and wore two bracelets on her left hand, silver and red. Meredith wore a purple striped shirt with boots and a cowboy hat and was standing by Rebekah who wore a yellow dress with pink flowers on it and yellow high heels. Rebekah's hair was curled, but Jameson knew it would straighten back up later. Rebekah's hair never stayed curled. Will wore a camo jacket and blue jeans with black sneakers and a camo baseball hat too. They were an eclectic group, but Jameson was grateful he had them.

Kids and teachers kept pouring into the gym. Jameson saw Becky and Carl walk in and waved at them. Becky and Carl were brother and sister. Jameson waved at Mrs. Jacky and his math teacher, Mrs. Ginger. He said hello to Mr. Rogers as well.

Walking up to the DJ, Jameson requested some country music. The DJ turned on the speakers and music blared. It was Jameson's favorite song, Country Boy. The song made him feel happy because his grandfather used to sing it all the time while he was working in his shop. His grandpa died a couple of years ago after a stroke, but this song always made him happy.

Jameson and his friends stepped onto the dance floor and started dancing. Rebekah did some cool gymnastics moves and Will started to do some hip-hop dances. Meredith went over to the concession stand and came back with chocolate bars for everyone. Jameson and Cindy went over to a booth by the snack stand and picked out glow sticks for all their friends.

With Jameson and his friends on the dance floor, soon, everyone else gathered on the floor and started dancing too. The disco ball lit and started spinning, refracting little spots of light across the gym. The lights dimmed and everyone knew it was time for the most romantic part of the dance. The DJ turned on a slow dance. Everyone found a partner and started dancing. Jameson partnered up with Rebekah. Will paired up with Cindy and Meredith pulled Carl from the concession stand line to dance. Becky had found a boy in 7th grade to dance with, so Jameson didn't know his name.

After a minute or two, the music ended, and everyone started getting snacks, drinks, and glow sticks.

"Jameson, come over here for a second!" Mr. Rogers called over from the concession stand.

Jameson ran over to Mr. Rogers. Mr. Rogers was wearing a light green long sleeve collared shirt and blue jeans. He was also wearing some fancy alligator skin boots. Jameson wished he had boots like that. He had never seen anything like them.

"We have too many coke cans that were donated tonight and we're trying to get rid of a few of them before this dance ends. Do you want one? They're free!" Mr. Rogers asked.

"Sure." Jameson said as he took the coke from Mr. Rogers. Jameson realized suddenly that the free drink was in his dream too, but pushed the thought away.

Meredith called Jameson back over to the group.

"I've got to go. Thank you, Mr. Rogers!" Jameson exclaimed as he ran back over to his friends.

Will and Rebekah started whacking each other with the glow sticks that Jameson and Cindy had brought to them. After hitting each other for a while, of course, one accidentally hit Meredith, so she got in on the glow stick fight. Eventually, Will's glow stick broke and started sparking. Will asked, "Should I throw it in those cardboard boxes by the concession stand?"

"No! It will start a fire!" Jameson quickly answered, "I'm sure of it."

"Don't be so scared, Jameson. If so, the teachers will see the fire and put it out quickly. We won't say anything and act like we had nothing to do with it. The fire would be cool to watch too." Meredith said.

"This is a bad idea. What if it gets too big too fast? What if the teachers can't control it?" Jameson asked, "You may be risking people's lives."

"Yea, Meredith. It's a bad idea." Rebekah agreed with Jameson.

"I think we should just throw it in the trash can and listen to Jameson." Cindy said, "The fire could light the wooden roof on fire if it gets too high."

"Fine. We will just put it in the trash can." Will said as he threw it in the trash.

"Now, let's have some fun!" Cindy screamed, loud enough for the whole gym to hear. Everyone crowded on the dance floor and started dancing to the funky beat that was playing.

All was going great until the plastic trash can that Will put the glow stick in, exploded in a column of flames. Everyone gasped and stepped back. Mrs. Ginger ran over with an extinguisher and tried to put out the fire, but the fire was already too big. The fire melted the plastic and the hot liquid oozed onto the cardboard boxes. The boxes quickly caught fire next, setting the concession stand ablaze as well. Mr. Rogers ran outside screaming as he tried to put out the spot of fire on his blazer. The fire spread up the wooden walls and to the ceiling where debris started to fall.

"This is exactly like my dream." Jameson whispered to himself.

Jameson saw Mrs. Jacky running to the door, but about halfway there, a chunk of wood from the ceiling fell on her.

"Mrs. Jacky!!" Jameson cried out, "No!!"

Everyone panicked and screamed as smoke filled the building and wood and metal beams fell from the ceiling. Jameson and his friends ran for the door, but just before the got there, a huge chunk of wood fell in front of the door, blocking the only exit.

"What are we going to do?" Meredith asked.

"I don't-" Jameson's words were interrupted by the loud screeching of metal against metal. Jameson looked up just in time to see the metal beam falling right above he and his friends. Jameson grabbed Meredith and Will and leaped forward. They landed with a big crash.

"Owwwww!!" Meredith yelled.

Jameson looked up and found that they had landed on top of Becky and Carl. Jameson remembered Becky's straightened hair when he waved at her earlier, but it was now a mess of frizzy knots and loops. Becky's jeans were torn and she was shaking, most likely from shock. Carl's face was black with smoke and his shirt was stained with blood. He was clearly hurt.

Jameson turned around to see that the beam had fallen on his good friends, Rebekah and Cindy.

"No!!" Meredith yelled as she sat on the floor.

"Why?!?" Will screamed.

Becky started crying and Jameson fell to his knees. "If I hadn't told you to throw the glow stick in the trash can, none of this would have happened. We should have asked an adult what to do!" Jameson said to Will.

Will sniffled, "It's not your fault. If we had asked the teachers, I'm pretty sure that they would have said to throw it in the trash too."

The fire kept raging around them and kids kept screaming and running around. Suddenly, a loud cracking sound echoed across the room. Jameson looked over in the direction of the sound and immediately, the wall fell through. All the smoke floated out into the open night air. The fire department rushed in and put out the fires with their powerful hoses.

Jameson went home that night and cried himself to sleep. His mom had tried to talk to him, but Jameson had pushed her away. His mom respected his space and left him alone in his room. A total of 16 people had died in the fire and 3 of those were Jameson's good friends. Mr. Rogers had minor burns and Carl had a bad cut on his back. Will went to the hospital for smoke inhalation. Meredith, Becky, and Jameson were fine physically. They had been lucky.

Jameson couldn't stop thinking that if he had never told Will to throw the glow stick away, the fire would have never started. He had dreamed this but didn't use the dream to protect his friends because he hadn't believed. He vowed to himself never to let this happen again.

Chapter 10

Jameson woke up to the smell of homemade waffles. He dressed and walked downstairs to find his mom in the kitchen cooking blueberry waffles and sausage. Jameson loved waffles.

Today, his mom wore a black dress with white stripes and black high heels for church. Jameson wore a navy-blue collared shirt with khaki pants and boots. He had known his mom would expect to attend church today.

"Come eat some waffles." Holly said.

"Mom, my dream came true! Are we seriously going to act like nothing happened?" Jameson yelled.

"It was just a coincidence." Holly said calmly.

"A coincidence? A coincidence? That was not a coincidence, mom! That was like....... powers or maybe I just had a glimpse into the future! There is something wrong with me!" Jameson yelled, even louder than last time. He pushed back from the table and began to pace.

"It's time we have a talk, Jameson....... about your dad *and* your dreams." his mom said sternly and quietly.

"What does dad have to do with my dreams?" Jameson stopped pacing to look at his mom.

"That's what I am about to answer." Holly said.

"I have powers, don't I?" Jameson whispered.

His mom sighed, "Yes. You were born with this special power gifted by a wizard. I know it doesn't make sense, but just listen to me until I'm done."

She put her hand on Jameson's shoulder and firmly guided him to a chair. "When you dream, your dream comes true. You can dream of anything. You can dream of a unicorn and a unicorn will show up on your doorstep. You can dream of gold and you will wake up with piles of gold laying around your room. You can dream of a car crash and a car wreck will happen on your street. You have a great power. But there is one catch, you can't dream people back from the dead." Holly told Jameson.

"So, I can't dream Dad, Cindy, Rebekah, or Mrs. Jacky back?" Jameson asked.

"No, sweetie, you can't." Holly answered.

"Did my dreams kill Dad?!?" Jameson asked, jumping to conclusions.

"Honey, I'm so sorry…" his mom whispered.

"What happened to him? You told me, years ago, when I asked, that he died of a heart attack! You lied to me!" Jameson shouted.

"Jameson, sweetie, it was for your own good!" Holly said sternly.

"How did Dad die?!?" Jameson screamed.

Jameson's mom was crying now, "You dreamt of a cyclops and it killed your dad at the hospital. I had forgotten your dreamcatcher in the rush, so we didn't have it. That dreamcatcher has powers itself and worked to deter any of your dreams from coming true. You were never a child that suffered from nightmares or being afraid of the dark, but the dreamcatcher ceased to work when you turned 11. I was supposed to have taught you to have only good dreams or control your dreams by your birthday, but without your dad…it was hard."

"I can't believe you didn't tell me any of this!" Jameson shouted.

"Again, it was for your own good!" his mom cried.

"No. It wasn't, but this is!" Jameson stood suddenly and ran to his front door, opened it, and ran out.

"Jameson, come back! Come back here!" his mom started crying and leaned against the open door, "Please, come back. I'm sorry!"

Chapter 11

Jameson walked down the railroad tracks, cold and shivering. He couldn't believe his mom had lied to him! She had kept secrets from him for years! He definitely had a difficult time believing he had powers, but if this was real, he needed to learn to control his dreams. Jameson had been gone over night already. He had dreamed of a huge scoop of ice cream on purpose by thinking a lot about ice cream before he fell asleep and he awoke to the sound of an ice cream truck by the grocery store where he slept. The driver of the truck had given him a big free scoop of vanilla ice cream (probably because the driver thought Jameson was homeless). It was a Monday and school was canceled for the whole week because of the fire and for families in their close-knit community to grieve.

Jameson had run away from home because he was mad at his mom. When he was running down the street, he had thought it was a great idea, but now, he wanted to return home. He missed his mom. That was why he found himself walking down the train tracks. The railroad led back to his house.

Jameson was wondering what he would tell his mom when he heard a train headed toward him down the track. Jameson stared at the train as it got closer. The train didn't slow down. The train was probably ten feet away when Jameson leaped to the side and the train sped past. The train would have run over him. It never braked.

Jameson had the terrible fortune of landing in a thorny bush. When he stood up, a spider jumped on him. It was black with green stripes and was huge! It crawled up his arm and into his shirt.

"AAAHHH!!" Jameson screamed. The spider bit him on the chest and fell off into the grass.

Jameson looked up and saw that he was in front of his road. He walked down the road and to his driveway. He walked up the stone path to his house, still shaken by the spider, and knocked on the door.

Jameson's mom opened the door. She saw that it was Jameson and immediately shed tears of joy. She wrapped him in a big hug and brought him inside.

Holly smiled through her tears, "Jameson!?! You're back!"

"I understand why you didn't tell me. You were just protecting me. I'm so sorry I ran away. I love you so much." Jameson profusely apologized.

"It's okay. I'm sorry I didn't tell you about your dad and your powers sooner. I love you so much." his mom said.

They walked into the dining room where Holly prepared a dinner of steak and asparagus in celebration. They both sat down, smiled at each other, and started eating. After they finished, Jameson walked to bed. He brushed his teeth, changed into pajamas, and crawled into bed. His mom came in and tucked him in.

"Goodnight, Jameson. I love you." Holly whispered.

"I love you too. Goodnight. I'm glad to be home with you." Jameson whispered back as his mom walked out of the room.

Jameson pulled out his phone and called Becky.

"Hey, Beck! I'm just calling to check in. How's your brother?" Jameson asked.

"He's doing good. The cut on his back is healing really well. It still hurts for him to turn, but he can stand, sit, walk, and run." Becky answered.

"That's great. Glad that he is doing good. How are you doing?" Jameson asked.

"I'm watching TV right now. We were visiting Carl in the hospital today. He gets out in two more days." Becky said.

"That's good. I'm sure he was glad you all came by for a visit." Jameson assured Becky.

"Well, it's been great talking to you." Becky said, "I'll talk to you later."

"Ok." Jameson said, "Bye, Becky."

Jameson hung up and dialed in Meredith's number.

Meredith picked up the phone and squealed, "Hey, Jameson!!"

"Hey, Meredith. How are you doing?" Jameson wondered.

"I'm doing good. My family and I are on vacation since school is canceled this week. We're going to go hiking tomorrow. I'm super excited!" Meredith said.

"Good. Sounds fun!" Jameson said jealously, "Where are you all?"

"We're in Ohio. It's really beautiful up here. I love all the trees and their different colors." Meredith replied.

"Glad you're liking it. We're all good down here. Nothing big happening in town." Jameson stated, "I'll call you later."

"Okeydokey." Meredith said a little too loudly, "I'll call you later."

"Bye." Jameson said as he pressed the red button and hung up. Jameson set his phone on his nightstand and plugged it into the charger.

Jameson turned over and closed his eyes. He fell asleep and started to dream. Tonight, he didn't dream of anything bad though. He dreamt of gold, lots and lots of gold.

Chapter 12

Jameson woke up and sat up to place his feet on the floor. As he stood, his feet felt something cold and hard. He turned on the lights and saw a mound of 6 gold bars on his floor. He was in shock. He couldn't speak. He had *gold* sitting on his floor.

"Mom!! Mom!!" Jameson screamed.

"What!?!" his mom yelled as she walked through the door.

"What. Is. That." Holly stared in awe.

"I had a dream about gold and this appeared." Jameson answered.

"What are we going to do with it?" Holly asked.

"Put it towards college. After all, it *is* my dream." Jameson said.

"I'll go to the bank today to put it in your college savings account. Do you want to come with me?" Holly asked.

"Sure!" Jameson replied.

They quickly got dressed and made breakfast. Holly pulled out cereal and poured in some milk. Jameson and Holly gobbled it up and brushed their teeth.

After Holly finished brushing, she yelled, "I'll be in the car! Grab the gold on your way out!"

Jameson put up his toothbrush and toothpaste in his bathroom drawer. He put his phone in his pocket and walked over to the gold. He tried picking them all up at once and fell forward.

"Ow." Jameson said as he got up and dusted himself off.

The gold was heavier than he had thought. He would have to pick one up at a time. He grabbed the brick on the top of the stack and walked outside. He opened the car door and set down the bar.

"Where are the other bars?" his mom asked.

"They were too heavy." Jameson replied.

Over time, he grabbed the rest of the gold by bringing them out to the car one by one. He finally climbed in and they drove to the bank.

Once they arrived at the bank, they drove into the drop-off area. They put one gold bar in the carrier in the pipe and the bank sucked it up. They saw the bank lady receive it through the window and she stared at the bar in awe.

The speaker at their private drive-thru spot turned on and they heard the lady's voice, "Where did you get this?"

"We were in Egypt on vacation and stumbled into an ancient cemetery. We found a coffin and there were piles of gold lying around it. We called an archeologist and they said that we could keep the gold since we were the people to find it." Holly lied.

"That's pretty cool!" said the lady on the speaker, "You can send up the rest."

The carrier came back down the tube and Holly sent up the bars one at a time.

"What account would you like to put this in?" asked the lady.

"Put it in Jameson's college savings account please." Holly said with a smile.

"I will do that." said the lady, "Have a good day!"

"You too!" Holly said as they drove away.

They arrived back to the house thirty minutes later and began preparing lunch. Jameson made he and his mom some peanut butter and jelly sandwiches and they sat down in the living room to watch TV. Holly turned on the news as Jameson chowed down on his sandwich.

"Can I invite Will over to play today?" Jameson asked, "He's home from the hospital and I haven't seen him in forever. Today is the perfect time."

"Sure, sweetie. It'll be good to be together and talk." Holly answered.

"I'm calling him right now." Jameson said. He dialed Will's number and Will answered.

"Hey, dude. How's it going?" Will asked.

"Good. Hey, do want to come hang out today? My mom says it's fine and we could go swimming and play video games." Jameson assured Will.

"Isn't it too cold to be swimming?" asked Will.

"We can heat up the pool with the heaters." Jameson said.

"Okay. Sounds awesome!" Will said, "I'm riding my bike over right now."

It took five minutes for Will to get to Jameson's house. When he arrived, Jameson opened the door.

"Hey, buddy!!" Will yelled.

"What's up?" Jameson replied as they did their secret handshake.

Jameson's mom walked out of the kitchen with chocolate chip cookies and handed them to Jameson and Will.

"You both have fun. I already turned on the heater for the pool and attached the internet to the gaming console. I'll be in my room doing laundry." Holly said as she waved goodbye and headed off to the heaping pile of clothing sitting on the couch.

"First one to the pool wins!" Will yelled as he started running to the backdoor.

Jameson followed short behind. They opened the backdoor and ran like cheetahs. Will and Jameson made two big cannonballs in the pool, splashing the couch and chairs in the outdoor kitchen. They came up for air and stood in the shallow end.

"How are Meredith and Becky?" Will asked, "I know they made it out of the fire okay, but have you talked to them lately?"

"I talked to them both on FaceTime last night." Jameson answered, "They both said they were doing fine. Becky's brother, Carl, is still in the hospital but is being released tomorrow. The cut on his back is healing well. Meredith is in Ohio on vacation with her family. They are going hiking today."

"Good. I'm ready to see Carl's face again. It sounds like Meredith is having fun." Will said.

"How is Mr. Rogers?" Jameson asked, "I heard that he was in the same hospital as you."

"When I was there, I looked in his window and saw that he was wrapped pretty well with bandages. The nurses wouldn't let me in his room to talk, but when he saw me, he did wave at me and wink. I don't know when he gets out."

"Yeah. I agree." Jameson said with a smile, glad to hear that his friends were doing as well as they could be. He still felt guilty that so much of their pain was his fault, but he also knew that he needed to move forward.

"Do you want to go inside and play video games?" Jameson asked.

"Of course!" Will replied.

They both crawled out of the water and dried off with towels. They ran into the living room and turned on Paratrooper. Paratrooper was their favorite game. You were a soldier and had to shoot paratroopers out of the sky. Will always lost, but they enjoyed playing the game together. Their mom called them from the kitchen after an hour of games to come eat dinner. They put up the video game controllers and ran into the dining room. Holly had ordered pepperoni pizza with cheese bread. Will and Jameson set out napkins and poured drinks. Holly, Will, and Jameson sat down and began eating. Will grabbed two slices of pizza and one piece of bread. Jameson just started with one piece of bread and one slice of pizza. They finished their meal and Will's mom called Will on the phone to come home. Jameson waved goodbye as Will hopped on his bike to head home.

"That was awesome." Jameson said.

"I'm glad you had fun." said his mom as she started to put away the dishes and plates.

Jameson helped his mom with the dishes and they both went to bed. It had been a long day and Jameson fell fast asleep.

That night, Jameson dreamt of spiders....... millions of them.

Chapter 13

Jameson woke up to the sound of the oven timer beeping. He dressed and ran down the stairs and into the kitchen. Today his mom was pulling freshly baked strawberry muffins out of the oven. The smell was delightful. It smelled of freshly picked strawberries and homemade bread. Jameson walked over to his mom and gave her a big bear hug.

"Well, good morning!" his mom said.

Jameson's stomach rumbled, "Is it time to eat? Those muffins look heavenly."

"Why, thank you! Yes, it is time to eat. I have milk and butter sitting on the table. I made one batch of blueberry muffins and one batch of strawberry muffins. Believe me, they're delicious. I've already eaten two muffins." Holly laughed.

Today, Jameson's mom was wearing a red shirt and khaki shorts. Her auburn hair was in a bun and she wore her red sandals.

"You look nice today." Jameson commented.

"Thank you!" his mom said, "Now eat your breakfast."

Jameson sat down with his mom at the perfectly prepared table. The baskets of muffins were in the middle of the table and butter and milk were at each of their spots. The napkins and silverware were laid neatly on the table in their correct positions. Clearly, his mom had done a lot to make this breakfast perfect.

"So, Mom, have you seen any spiders in our house this morning?" Jameson asked.

"No. Why? Did you have a dream?" Holly asked cautiously.

"Yes, and it was terrible. Spiders the size of golf balls surrounded you and crawled on top of you. They overtook you and you fell to the ground. They were poisonous and bit you in a hundred different places. You died." Jameson explained, whispering the last part.

"Oh. Well, in that case, we better get the spider spray out." Jameson's mom tried laughing and then got serious, "Your dreams are powerful and will always come true unless you stop them. *You* are the only one who can stop your dreams from happening."

"So, you mean, if I spray the spiders or squish them, they won't kill you? I could stop the dream from happening? I thought my dreams happened no matter what." Jameson wondered.

"Yes, that is exactly what I mean." Jameson's mom said, "If I see any spiders, I will tell you."

"Okay. Thanks, Mom." Jameson said, feeling helpful as he put his plate in the dish washer and ran to his room.

Jameson logged onto his favorite videogame, Destroyer, and started playing. He jumped over bombs and shot arrows at monsters. He climbed mountains and flew over valleys. It was his favorite game. Jameson lost track of time and played for three hours before he heard a piercing cry coming from the laundry room. It was his mom.

....

Jameson ran downstairs to the laundry room to find his mom covered in spiders. The spiders were red with blue dots, just like in Jameson's dream. They had already bitten her a couple of times and she was screaming and crying. She tried to squish them or scrape them off, but more kept coming.

Jameson ran outside and grabbed the hose to wash them away. He ran inside and sprayed his mom and all the spiders. The spiders that Jameson sprayed crumpled into golden dust, but more kept coming from every crack and hole in the house. Then, Jameson had a great idea. He ran to the shed and grabbed a five-gallon bucket full of water and took it to the laundry room. He poured the five gallons of water on his mom and the water splattered across the floor. Every spider that got close to his mom turned to dust.

"Mom, their weakness is water!" Jameson yelled.

"What?!? That's why the sprinklers turned the cyclops to dust at the hospital. Keep pouring!" Holly yelled.

Jameson laughed and ran outside to grab the hose. He ran back inside to his mom and just as he was turning on the hose, a red and blue spider the size of a TV jumped on him. Jameson grabbed the spider by the legs and flung it into the side of the washer machine. One hundred spiders crumpled to dust behind Jameson without being killed by water.

"Mom, if I hurt the big spider, some of the spiders die, so if I *kill* the big spider, *all* of the little ones die!" Jameson yelled.

"Great!" his mom screamed over the whistling of the millions of spiders around them.

Jameson's mom dove for the big spider as it tried to escape out the door. She grabbed the spider and threw it into the dryer. Jameson locked the machine's door and turned it on. The spider spun and spun and got hotter and hotter.

Finally, the spider stopped struggling and tossing around. The spider became still and lifeless. It had died.

"Woohoo! Yea!" Jameson jumped up and down.

"You did it, Jameson!" his mom yelled.

All around them, the spiders fell and disintegrated into golden flakes. Jameson had won. Jameson stopped his dream from turning into reality.

"Did you *have* to dream of spiders?" Holly laughed.

"I got bit by a spider on my way home the other night after I ran away. I guess it was why I dreamt of spiders." Jameson answered, just now realizing that the bites on he and his mom were gone. They had probably disappeared since the dream didn't happen.

"You actually stopped your dream from happening. I'm so proud of you." Jameson's mom congratulated as she hugged him tightly.

"I love you, Mom." Jameson said with a smile.

"I love you too." Holly said.

Holly and Jameson took the broom and mop and cleaned up the mess of shiny flakes together.

Jameson whispered to himself, "I guess I *can* stop my dreams."

Chapter 14

Jameson had dreamed of a snake last night. The snake was so big that it blocked out the sun. This had been his worst dream yet. Jameson was going to protect his home though. Jameson walked down the stairs to the kitchen to help his mom make bacon and eggs.

When he arrived, his mom had already done the eggs. Jameson got out the bacon and put it on the pan. The smell of bacon started to flow through the air.

"I had a dream last night, Mom. There was a huge snake and it attacked you." Jameson told his mom.

"We need to watch for snakes then." Holly said confidently.

"Okay. The bacon is ready." Jameson said as he got out plates and divided the food.

They both sat down and started eating. "So, what did this snake look like?"

"It was dark green and huge." Jameson said, "It crushed you as it wrapped you up."

"I'll get the hose as soon as I see a snake. If it's that big then I should see it easily." Holly promised.

"Okay. Be careful. It will be super dangerous." Jameson warned.

They finished breakfast and Jameson went to the pool to swim even though it was freezing. Jameson found that he liked swimming in cold water more than warm water. His mom went to shovel snow in the garden. Jameson grabbed a towel and some goggles. He laid his towel on a table in the outdoor kitchen and put his goggles on his head. He had done three laps around the pool when he heard a scream. It was coming from the garden.

....

Jameson's mom ran towards the pool screaming. Jameson watched her as she reached the outdoor kitchen, but something leaped from the ground behind her and wrapped around her body. It was a silver scaly snake about the size of car! It had fangs as sharp as knives and a glare that could turn you to stone. It squeezed Holly tighter and tighter until she couldn't breathe.

For a quick second, Jameson rolled his eyes and thought, "Why does this keep happening? First spiders, now snakes. My mom *must* need glasses." and then quickly jumped out of the pool to get the shovel that his mom had dropped. He charged the snake with the tool and gutted it. It screeched and started slithering away. It knocked over pots and chairs as it retreated to the plants behind the pool. Jameson ran over to his mom, who had been let loose by the snake, and grabbed her hand to help her off the ground. She grunted as she stood up and clutched her ribs. She was in no condition to help fight this monster.

"Mom, I thought you would tell me if you saw a snake!" Jameson said.

"I didn't see it. I was shoveling snow by the strawberries when the camouflaged snake leaped down from the pine tree by the muscadines. It slithered toward me and I ran. I obviously wasn't fast enough." Holly grunted. It was hard for her to talk through her pain.

"Hey, Mom! I have a plan." Jameson said, "I'm going to push the snake into the pool with our tractor, so it will disintegrate into ashes. You hide in your bedroom."

"Perfect!" Holly said with a forced smile across her face.

Holly hobbled inside through the backdoor and Jameson ran into the garage to get the tractor. Jameson opened the garage door and hopped on the tractor. The keys were still in the tractor from the last time they used it, so Jameson started the tractor and drove out the door.

He was driving directly towards the snake when it decided to stop waiting and to go for Jameson. It raised its head and slithered toward the tractor. It struck the vehicle and made a dent in the side. Jameson turned the tractor and whacked the snake in the head with the tractor bucket. The snake slithered over to the pool in the perfect position for Jameson to push it in. Jameson drove full speed ahead and rammed into the serpent. It fell in the pool and started shrieking. The snake thrashed as it slowly crumbled into golden flakes. The ashes were quickly sucked into the pool filter.

Jameson hopped off of the tractor and ran inside to find his mom. He took out his phone and called 9-1-1 for help.

....

An ambulance arrived and took he and his mom to the hospital. Four nurses took Holly away. Jameson waited in the hospital waiting room until a nurse told him that they were ready for him to go check on his mom. He walked down to the room and opened the door. His mom was in the bed wrapped in bandages around her waist. She had broken a total of four ribs. Jameson had to lie to the nurses about the incident. He said that she had fallen off a ladder cleaning the gutters. Jameson felt bad about the lie, but he knew he had to do it.

"Hey, Mom." Jameson said.

"Hey, sweetie. How's it going?" Holly asked.

"Good. I've been playing checkers and tic-tac-toe in the lounge. It's fun. How are you feeling?" Jameson wondered.

"I'm glad you had fun." Holly said with a smile, "I'm doing good. They said I'll be released soon, so we can go home."

"Good. I want us to be home together, but without all the snakes and spiders." Jameson said.

Holly chuckled, "Me too. Now you go watch TV in the lounge while I take a nap. I love you."

"I love you too, Mom." Jameson said as he hugged his mom and walked back to his room.

Holly was released from the hospital two days later. Jameson had slept on the lounge couch the past two days and was really tired. He was excited to get back home to his own bed. They both returned home and cleaned up the house and yard. They worked together to replace pots and put back chairs. They also had to clean out the pool filters since the golden flakes had filled them up. They put back the tractor and Holly finished shoveling the garden's snow.

They finished all of the cleaning and went inside to relax. After they turned on the TV in the living room, they both sat down on the couch.

"Thanks for taking charge when the snake attacked me." Holly said.

"Your welcome. I'm glad you're okay. It's hard, but I am going to learn to control this gift." Jameson replied.

"Your idea to kill the snake was really smart. I'm proud of you and have faith in you. Now, do you want to watch Five Star Restaurant? It's about this couple who goes around the world trying food from every 5-star restaurant." Holly recommended, "It's pretty awesome."

"Sounds good, Mom." Jameson said, "I love you."

"I love you too, honey." Holly said as she hugged her child.

Chapter 15

1 Week Later

Life was great. Jameson had learned to control his powers fully by concentrating on the positive things in the world and being mindful of what his last thoughts were before he went to sleep. One night, Jameson had dreamt of gifts, food, and his family coming over for a big party. The next day, his aunt and uncle, his cousins, and his grandparents came over to his house for a Christmas gathering, just as in his dream.

Jameson's grandparents, cousins, aunt, and uncle brought food and presents. Jameson's grandma had made deviled eggs and his grandpa brought turkey. After everyone had settled in, Jameson and his cousins played in the snow by building snowmen. They also had a snowball fight where everyone ended up cold, wet, but happy. They went back inside and played the video games Paratrooper and Tornado. Shirley and Lucas were his cousin's names and Shirley was a very sore loser when she lost at Paratrooper. They watched a couple of movies and then went to eat turkey, biscuits (made by his mom), and deviled eggs with their family.

After dinner, Jameson's mom and grandparents cleaned up the dining room and kitchen. Jameson washed his hands and quickly ran to the living room where his cousins, aunt, and uncle were waiting to open gifts.

Jameson's mom and grandparents joined the rest of the family and they started opening presents. The presents were all wrapped in matching gold, red, and green patterns. Jameson opened his presents first and received a new phone, a pool float for their pool, cologne, and a book series that he had really wanted to read. He received everything he had dreamt in his dream the night before. Knowing what he was going to receive because of his dream *did* spoil the surprise, but Jameson was fine with it because it confirmed he was gaining control of his power. After everyone else opened their gifts, Jameson could tell that everyone was very happy with their presents because of the contented smiles and easy natures within the home.

Everyone left Jameson's house happy and content that night toward their own homes. Jameson and his mom cleaned up around the house. The dishes were cleaned, as was the wrapping paper and all the toys that the younger cousins had pulled out of Jameson's room.

As Jameson's mom put up the last toy, she said, "Thank you so much for being so gentle and sweet with your cousins. I know you don't have anyone your age to play with in our family, but you get along pretty well with them."

"Thanks, Mom. I enjoy hanging out with them. Today they built a really cool snowman." Jameson said, as he pointed out the window at the snowy figure.

The snowman was big. It's head and body were perfectly rounded, and it had three black buttons going up its body. It wore a silk black hat and had a corn cob pipe. It had a carrot nose and eyes made of coal. Its smile was warm and gave you good feelings when you looked at it.

"It looks amazing!" Holly commented.

"I know. The cousins were very proud of themselves." Jameson said.

"Great. Now wash that last dish and get to bed. I had a lot of fun today. I love you. Goodnight." Jameson's mom said as she walked off to bed.

"Okay. I had fun too. I am just thankful to have an event that was not ruined because of a dream I had. I feel like I am finally able to control this power. I love you too. Goodnight." Jameson said as he put the last plate in the dish washer and went to bed.

Chapter 16

26 Years Later

"Christie, have you seen my wallet?" Jameson called out from across the house.

"No! Check your pants and check the car!" Christie shouted.

"Okay! Thanks! I will!" Jameson thanked.

After high school, Jameson attended Weston University in his hometown so he could be close to his family. When he left college, he attained a job at a local animal hospital. He met a woman named Christie and took her as his bride. They loved each other very much. Christian and Gabel were the two sons that made their family complete. The boys both had blonde hair and blue eyes. They both loved basketball and liked to go fishing with their father in their free time. They weren't twins, though they looked very much alike. Christian was one year older than Gabel. Christie was a school teacher at Weston Elementary where both boys attended. While at work, Jameson tended to the community's dogs, horses, cows, and cats every day. Christian and Gabel liked their dad's job because sometimes they were allowed to go to his work to pet and bathe some of the animals.

Jameson's mom still lived in Weston. She came and visited almost every weekend and attended every one of the boys' basketball and fishing competitions. She loved helping the boys with their homework and bringing them cookies and brownies. Holly had been very happy when she learned she was going to be a grandparent and had called Christie after every one of her pregnancy appointments to check on her. Their families were very close and were made closer by the secret they all kept for Jameson.

For dinner, Christie had made pork loin and broccoli. She had also picked some peaches from their little orchard for them to eat. It was mid-summer, and everyone was either outside swimming in their pools or at the beach. Christian and Gabel joined Jameson and Christie in the kitchen and together, they ate the feast.

Jameson had told his wife and children about his power, but not the town. He didn't want to risk the safety of his mom, wife, or children if others became too curious or would try to manipulate Jameson's power for themselves. By keeping his power secret, they remained very happy and blessed as a family.

Of course, Jameson still had the usual dreams. He would dream of a delicious dinner and they had burgers and sausage the next night. He dreamed of a sunny day and the next day, the sky shone brightly. Jameson wondered if his powers were hereditary and wondered if his sons would grow to discover powers too. He wouldn't worry if they did get powers because he would teach them before anything terrible happened. Even if his kids dreamt something terrible, Jameson was ready. He had been through the same thing before and felt more prepared than ever to take care of his wife and children.

After the delicious dinner, Christie washed dishes and Jameson brought the kids to bed. Jameson watched as his children brushed their teeth and headed off to their rooms. He tucked both of them in snuggly and gave them each a hug. Jameson turned out the lights and went downstairs to go to sleep. On Jameson's way down stairs, he almost tripped over a yellow toy truck. As he regained his balance, he grabbed the truck and set it on a table. Jameson thought about his kids and how much he loved them. The days that Christian and Gabel were born were truly some of the happiest days of Jameson's life.

Jameson walked to bed and found that Christie was already asleep. Jameson brushed his teeth, crawled into bed, and closed his eyes.

....

Meanwhile, in Christian's room, Christian lay wide awake. He wondered if he would ever have a sister to play with on his family's big and amazing property. That would be fun! He hoped that was what his dad would dream of soon. His dad told him that perhaps it might be possible for one of the boys to display the same power as their dad, but this had not happened yet.

Christian's brother, Gabel, was already asleep. Christian could hear Gabel's loud snoring from the other room.

Christian's eyes started to close, and he let them. He cuddled up with his fluffy teddy bear and fell asleep.

Soon, Christian had a dream....... A dream of a baby sister.......

CPSIA information can be obtained
at www.ICGtesting.com
Printed in the USA
LVHW010623220221
679516LV00006B/512